# The Wonderful Adventures of

# BRADLEY THE BAT

## Written by Steve Paulding
## Illustrated by Caleb and Carter Schmidt

Design by
Concepts Unlimited
www.ConceptsUnlimitedInc.com

Published by

Slow on the Draw
PRODUCTIONS
LifeLessonsFromAndyWink.com

12826 Ironside Way, #304
Parker, CO 80134
www.LifeLessonsFromAndyWink.com

ISBN:  978-0-615-74591-6          (pbk)

13    14    15    16    17          0  9  8  7  6  5  4  3  2  1

Printed in the USA

## Special Thanks

To Mom and Dad for their continued support!

To Carter and Caleb for their wonderful illustrations!

To Stephanie and Brian for loaning out Carter and Caleb so they could draw their wonderful illustrations!

To Mrs. Burden's 2011-2012 fourth grade class for inspiring me!

*Once upon a time there lived a little brown bat named Bradley.*

Bradley lived in the state of Colorado, by the foothills of the Rockies, in the rafters of an old red barn.

Bradley lived with his father Ben, his mother Blair, and his grandpa Broderick.

One evening before Bradley's family flew off in search of their dinner, Bradley wanted to make a very important announcement, but no one seemed to be listening.

"Could I have your attention please?" Bradley asked. "I said, could I have your attention please?"

"I think I'll fly over the lake tonight," Bradley's mother stated. "I noticed several different species of tasty insects there the other night."

"Mom," Bradley interrupted. "Instead of hibernating this year, I think I'd like to..."

"Bradley, don't interrupt your mother," scolded Bradley's father.

Bradley's mother continued.

"Moths, beetles, other types of insects…"

"I think my aerial hawking and gleaming tactics were off last night. I guess that's what happens when you get older," commented Broderick.

"Dad, your swooping and dipping maneuvers are fine," Ben said to his father.

"Grandpa?" Bradley continued, "Since I'm a temperate bat, I think instead of hibernating in the cave this winter, I'd like to…"

"And my echolocation's off," Broderick continued, "I don't hear like I used to."

"Your hearing's fine Dad," Ben whispered into his father's ear.

"Why won't anyone listen to me?" Bradley shouted!

"Bradley," scolded his mother, "if you don't stop interrupting I'm going to send you to bed without any supper!"

"What are you trying to say, son?  We're listening."

All of the bat family was quiet, waiting to see what Bradley had to say.

"I think instead of hibernating in the cave this winter, I'd like to migrate to South America...where it's warmer."

"Why would you want to do a thing like that?" asked Bradley's mother. "We have a perfectly warm cave here! We hibernate in it every winter."

"There's too much bat guano!" Bradley laughed out loud as he rolled on a beam.

"Bradley, that's not an appropriate thing to say," scolded Bradley's father. "We've hibernated in that cave as long as I can remember."

"He's right," Grandpa Broderick said, laughing with Bradley, "There are thousands of bats that live there, and it is awfully deep!"

Bradley laughed even louder!

"Dad, stop egging him on!"

"I won't hear of it," interrupted Bradley's mother. "It's too dangerous!"

"But Mom," Bradley pleaded, "I want to see what's out there! This winter I want to go where it's warm, like Mexico or South America!"

"Bradley, you heard your mother."

"But Dad! I'm tired of this old barn and I'm tired of hibernating in that old cave!"

"This barn and that cave are our homes. Don't you think you'd miss them if they weren't here?"

Bradley thought for a moment.

"Yes, Sir," Bradley answered remorsefully.

"I migrated to Mexico and South America when I was Bradley's age," Grandpa Broderick commented. "I think we should think it over. As long as he stays safe and doesn't talk to strangers, I don't see anything wrong with it."

Grandpa Broderick winked at Bradley.

*Bradley's family talked for over an hour about Bradley's trip.*

After much deliberation, the family decided to let Bradley go. Bradley could hardly wait to tell his best friend Brayden!

"I can't believe you're leaving," Brayden shouted, as he swooped down on a bug. "That's awesome!"

"I just want to see what's out there," Bradley replied, swooping around his friend.

"It's going to be a long haul," Brayden commented, as he landed and hung upside down from a branch of their thinking tree. "South America's a long way away! Aren't you scared?"

"Not really," Bradley answered. "My grandpa says there's just as much danger for a brown bat in Mexico or South America as there is in Colorado."

"Won't you miss your family?"

A full moon crept slowly over the hillside.

"I'll see them again," commented Bradley as he hung next to Brayden. "I love hanging in our thinking tree and watching the moon come up!"

"It makes the night look like day," shouted Brayden, "and we hardly ever get to see day!"

"I like it because we can catch more bugs for our dinner," cheered Bradley as he swooped around his friend.

"Hey Bradley," Brayden asked. "What do you get when you cross a bat with a ball?"

"A homerun!"

Bradley and Brayden laughed out loud as they swooped and dove for insects in front of the moon.

Early the next evening Bradley said goodbye to his family and Brayden, and headed south.

After flying for what seemed forever, Bradley realized that what Brayden had said was true. It was going to be a very long haul.

Bradley spotted a huge cave below which looked like it was surrounded by rows and rows of seats. He decided to take a break and rest. As he flew into the cave he noticed thousands of bats getting ready for what seemed like a performance.

"What's your name?" A young bat asked Bradley.

"I'm Bradley, Bradley the bat! What's your name?"

"I'm Barclay," he answered doing several flips in the air, "I'm an acting bat!"

"An acting bat, what's that?"

"We're all acting bats," Barclay continued, motioning to the other bats in the cave, "we perform every night here at Carlsbad."

"Carlsbad? What's Carlsbad and what do you perform?"

"Carlsbad Caverns National Park, it's where you are. Every night hundreds of people come to watch us fly out of this cave. We fly out in a huge group at sunset. There are so many of us it looks like a giant black cloud coming out of the cave! We dive, we swoop, and we do acrobatics! Get it? Acro 'bat'ics? And a park ranger gives a talk while the audience sits in an amphitheatre below us. Sometimes they play music while we're flying."

"Can I perform with you?" Bradley asked, his voice trembling with excitement.

"Sure! The more the merrier!"

As the sun began to set, Bradley listened as the music began to play. It was the most beautiful music he had ever heard.

"What music is this?" Bradley asked. "It's beautiful!"

"It's classical. It's written by a guy named Bruch. Symphony No. 2 in F Minor. They play classical music, sometimes they play rock and roll or jazz, sometimes they play music from movies. All of it's great to fly to! Now, when the music gets louder we go, got it? It's all very theatrical."

The music started to get louder, and louder, and louder.

"Here we go," Barclay shouted. "Are you ready?"

"Ready!" Bradley shouted back.

Bradley could hardly stand it. He was filled with such excitement!

He flew after Barclay, as thousands of bats flew out of the cave corkscrewing upwards into the sky and flying counterclockwise in front of the sunset.

The audience let out a gasp filled with amazement, which was followed by gigantic cheers, and whistles, and then massive applause.

Bradley and Barclay had the best time. They performed for hours well into the night. At the end of the performance the audience gave Bradley, Barclay, and the rest of the bats a standing ovation.

As the sun started to rise, Bradley and Barclay headed back to the cave.

"I think it's great that you're heading to South America! I've always wanted to go there."

"Why don't you come with me?" asked Bradley.

"I'd like to, but I can't. I can't miss a performance. We perform every night until early November."

"That's okay," Bradley answered, understanding. "Hey Barclay, thanks for letting me perform with you. I had a blast tonight!" "Anytime Bradley," Barclay answered yawning. "Now it's time for some rest!"

Bradley and Barclay hung upside down from the ceiling of the cave. They slowly fell asleep as their performance played back in their minds.

Early the next evening Bradley woke up and quietly flew out of the cave. He headed south as the sun began to set. As he flew, he wondered what kind of music Carlsbad would be playing tonight.

After many hours of flying, Bradley decided it was time to rest and have a snack.

*Bradley landed on what he thought was a tree, but it was fatter and had sharp, tiny needles sticking out of it.*

"Ouch!" Bradley screamed as he landed on one of the needles. "That hurt! What kind of a tree are you?"

"It's a prickly pear cactus," a voice said from the darkness.

"A what?" Bradley asked.

"A prickly pear cactus," the voice replied. "They grow all over Texas and Mexico."

"Who are you?" Bradley asked.

A blue morpho butterfly slowly fluttered out of the darkness.

"I'm a blue morpho butterfly; my name's Bella."

"Bella? What a beautiful name!" Bradley exclaimed.

It was obvious that Bradley had a crush on Bella.

"That's exactly what Bella means," Bella said floating through the air, "beautiful. What's your name?"

"I'm Bradley, Bradley the bat! I'm a little Colorado brown bat!"

"Well Bradley the bat, I hope you don't like to eat butterflies," Bella said, with a little concern in her voice.

"I love eating moths and butterflies and I am very hungry, but you're too beautiful to eat," Bradley explained. "I could never eat you! What kind of a butterfly are you?"

"I'm a Blue Morpho Butterfly. I'm wonderfully glossy and mesmerizing. I've been told that I'm the most beautiful butterfly in the world."

"You can say that again!" Bradley exclaimed.

"What brings you to Mexico, Bradley the bat?"

"I'm heading to South America to hibernate for the winter. It's warmer there!"

"That seems like a long way to go. Aren't there any warm places in Colorado where you can hibernate?" Bella asked.

"Just a smelly old cave," Bradley answered.

"Do you have any family?"

"I live with my mom and dad, and my grandpa. How about you?" Bradley asked, trying to float like Bella.

"I have thousands of brothers and sisters, but I don't see them much. I'm too busy traveling around the world."

"That's what I want to do. I want to see what's out there!"

"The world's a wonderful place Bradley, and there are so many amazing things to see and places to go. However, you've got to be careful. The world can also be a very dangerous place."

"That's what my grandpa told me," Bradley said, imitating his grandfather. "See the world Bradley, have fun, but stay safe."

"Your grandpa's a very smart bat. Take me for instance," Bella continued, "I could be eaten, get caught in a net, or end up in someone's butterfly collection!"

"I wouldn't like that!" exclaimed Bradley.

"Neither would I," agreed Bella.

Bradley went into deep thought as he flew through the air thinking about the places he'd like to travel to.

"Where have you been? I mean where have you traveled to?" Bradley asked.

"Well, I've traveled all over the United States."

"Have you ever been to Colorado?"

"Of course Bradley, I've been to Colorado several times. I've been to South America, and I've been to Europe."

"Europe, how did you fly all the way to Europe?"

"I didn't fly silly," Bella laughed, "I was a stowaway on a ship! No one seemed to mind. Someday I'd like to go to Africa."

"Africa? I've always wanted to go to Africa. I've heard it's beautiful!"

Bradley and Bella laughed as they sailed through the air. They flew through the night as Bella told wonderful stories about her travels and adventures. Finally, Bella landed on another cactus.

"Oh, no, you don't! The last time I landed on one of those things, I got stuck in my behind!"

"It's time for me to sleep Bradley. You're used to being up all night, but I need my rest."

"I guess this is goodbye," Bradley said sadly.

"It doesn't have to be," Bella replied. "Why don't we plan on going to Africa sometime?"

Bradley gasped with excitement.

"Together? You want to go to Africa with me? I'd like that!" Bradley exclaimed, full of happiness.

Bella flew to Bradley and gave him a little kiss on his nose.

"Safe travels Bradley. You're very handsome, for a bat."

And with that, Bella was gone. Bradley fluttered in the air for a moment and then realized what had just happened.

"I'm handsome!" Bradley shouted out loud. "She said I'm handsome!"

Bradley flew like a rocket through the air. He was filled with adrenalin as he headed south.

1

After many hours Bradley noticed something flickering on the ground. He flew closer to get a better look. Several small fires were burning outside of the shell of a giant animal. Bradley landed on a branch next to the shell. He had never seen anything like it!

The shell was long, had windows, and was made of metal. It was broken in pieces and half of the shell hung over a steep cliff.

"Who g-g-g-goes there?" A tiny voice squeaked from the other side of the shell.

"I'm Bradley, Bradley the bat. Who are you?"

A tiny bat about one inch long floated out of the darkness.

"I'm B-B-B-Billy, the B-B-B-Bumblebee Bat! I said who goes there?"

"I just told you who goes here. You're a what?"

"I'm a B-B-B-Bumblebee Bat!"

"You're not a bat, you're too small!"

"Who are you c-c-c-calling small?"

"I am."

"P-P-P-Put 'em up you big bully!"

Billy flew around Bradley lightly thumping him on the head.

"Cut that out!" Bradley said a little irritated. "You're too little to fight with. I'd feel like I was picking on you."

"P-P-P-Picking on me? Why I oughta!"

Bradley lightly pushed Billy out of the way and flew over the shell of the animal.

"What kind of an animal is this?" Bradley asked.

"It's n-n-n-not an animal," Billy replied. "It's an aeroplane!"

"A what?"

"An aeroplane! W-W-W-What are you, hard of hearing? You're a bat for g-g-g-goodness sakes!"

Bradley shot Billy an 'are you kidding me' look.

"I'm not hard of hearing. And you're acting awfully obnoxious for such a little spud!"

"S-S-S-Spud? Hey, that's a p-p-p-potato! Yer really getting on my noives!"

"What's an aeroplane , Billy?"

"It's s-s-s-something people fly in."

"What's it doing here?" Bradley asked.

"I don't kn-kn-kn-know, it's only been here a few days!"

"What's on the inside?"

"Just a b-b-b-bunch of straw and d-d-d-debris lying around. The p-p-p-pilots must have ej-j-j-jected before the aeroplane c-c-c-crashed! "

Bradley started to enter the aeroplane. Billy gasped out loud as he flew in front of Bradley trying to stop him from entering.

"Y-Y-Y-You don't w-w-w-want to go in t-t-t-there!"

"Why not? I'm not afraid!"

Billy gulped slowly. "Y-Y-Y-You will be," Billy whispered.

Bradley flew inside of the shell and looked around. There were bales of strange smelling straw strewn across the ground and a few posters lined the wall of the shell. Some of the posters were torn; some of them blew slowly in the wind. Bradley read the name on each poster as he flew by them.

"Black Sabbath, Rick James, Grateful Dead? I've never heard of them," commented Bradley.

Suddenly Bradley heard an elegant, impeccable sounding voice from the back of the shell.

"Well, well, well, Billy, what do we have here? Didn't his parents tell him to never stop and talk to strangers?"

"Looks like dinner," lisped another voice from the darkness.

Billy quickly flew inside the hollow shell and fluttered in front of Bradley. "I t-t-t-told him not to c-c-c-come in here Vic!"

Two odd looking bats entered from the darkness into the middle of the shell.

"That's Victor to you Bee!"

Victor grabbed Billy and threw him against the wall of the plane.

"I'm Victor the Vampire Bat," Victor announced with perfect pronunciation. "And this is my partner, in crime so to speak, Fabio, Fabio the Fruit Bat."

Bradley noticed that Fabio was wearing a robe and that it had flowers and butterflies on it. His head began to swoon at the thought of Bella.

"Hey, what kind of a robe is that?" asked Bradley. "It's got butterflies on it!"

"Robe? Fabio answered defensively. "This isn't a robe! It's a kimono! I got it in..."

"Enough with the conversation about fashion!" Victor said slowly, as he clamped Fabio's lips together with his claws. "I'm hungry. Why don't we find out what our little appetizer's doing in our jungle and on our aeroplane?"

"I'm on my way to South America!" Bradley replied.

"S-S-S-South America?" stammered Billy. "But he's already h-h-h-here!"

"Shouldn't you be outside standing guard?" Victor warned, grabbing Billy and throwing him out of a broken window.

"I think South America's that way," Victor said, elbowing Fabio in the ribs and pointing west.

"No it's not!" Fabio laughed taking the hint from Victor and pointing east, "It's that way!"

Fabio began to tickle Victor as the two bats pointed in every direction trying to confuse Bradley.

"Stop! Stop! Stop!" screamed Victor. "You know I can't stand being tickled!"

"Sorry boss," answered Fabio.

Billy flew back in through the window.

"I'm t-t-t-telling you he's already h-h-h-here."

"Out Bee!"

Victor grabbed Billy again and threw him out another window. "Hey! You're nothing but a bully!" yelled Bradley. "Why don't you pick on someone your own size?"

"How about I pick your flesh from my teeth?" Victor cackled as he grabbed Bradley.

"Let me go!" screamed Bradley!

Bradley bit Victor on the nose, which caused him to scream out loud and loosen his grip. Bradley flew from one side of the shell to the other. He flew out a window and was joined in flight by Billy.

"F-F-F-Fly Bradley, as far away from h-h-h-ere as you can! F-F-F-Fly Bradley! Fly!"

Billy's voice echoed through the darkness as Bradley flew south as fast and far as he could.

"Stay safe," Bradley remembered his grandpa saying. "Stay safe and don't talk to strangers!"

Bradley flew until everything below him was white.

"I'm freezing," Bradley said as his teeth began to chatter.

Bradley looked for a place he could use for shelter. He saw a small cave in the whiteness. He flew in, hung upside down, and tried to rest.

After many hours, Bradley woke up on the ground in a daze. He was wrapped in a small piece of blue cloth. He looked up and saw two strange-looking animals staring at him. One animal was tall and slender the other was short and a little heavy.

# "Wake up little buddy," the heavy animal stated.

"What?" Bradley asked groggily.

"He said to wake up old chap," replied the tall and slender animal.

"Who are you?" Bradley asked, a confused look on his face.

"I'm Pete the Emperor Penguin," replied the slender animal.

"And I'm Wally the Walrus," answered the heavier animal, "we found you on the ground of this cave. You almost froze to death!"

"What's this?" Bradley asked, as he wrapped the piece of cloth tighter around himself to keep warm.

"It's from the Palmer Research Station," commented Pete. "Their trash is always blowing around here."

"What's your name little buddy?" asked Wally.

"I'm Bradley, Bradley the bat! I was on my way to South America to hibernate, but I got into a little trouble along the way."

"Well you're far and away from South America little buddy," laughed Wally. "You've overshot it!"

"I say," commented Pete. "You've landed in Antarctica!"

"Antarctica? Where's Antarctica and what's that on your feet?" Bradley asked noticing an egg on the top off Pete's feet.

"Antarctica's on the bottom of the Earth," replied Pete . "And this is my offspring. I'm a stay-at-home dad."

"Stay-at-home dad? I don't understand," commented Bradley.

"Well, I take care of our egg while my wife is gone. I keep the egg warm with this special fold of skin that's under my tummy."

"Where's your wife?" asked Bradley.

"She's off looking for food in the ocean. She'll be back next month, when our egg hatches."

"Next month?" asked Bradley.

"Uh huh. She'll come back next month and feed our chick regurgitated fish."

"Regurgitated? What's that?" asked Bradley.

"Throw up," answered Wally.

"That's gross," commented Bradley.

"That's what I say," agreed Wally.

"And what do you do and where do you live?" asked Bradley, flying around Wally. "Your teeth are huge!"

"They're tusks little buddy. I live north of Greenland. But this time of year I swim down and spend time with my friend Pete to keep him company. Where are you from little buddy?"

"I'm from Colorado."

Pete and Wally look at each other, a look of concern on their faces.

"And how did you end up here?" asked Pete.

"Well like I said, I wanted to fly to South America to hibernate, where it's warmer," Bradley answered flying to Pete and hanging upside down from his beak. "But I ran into a couple of bats in South America and they told me to fly here."

"Didn't they know you could die down here?"

"Probably," Bradley answered. "They weren't very nice bats."

"Where's your family?" Wally asked.

"They're back in Colorado," Bradley answered.

"Bradley, I'm afraid we've got some bad news," Pete said sadly.

"What is it?" Bradley asked playfully tapping on Wally's tusks.

"We've heard through the animal kingdom that a plague's been spreading through the western part of the United States," explained Pete.

"What's a plague?" asked Bradley.

"It's a disease Bradley. This is a fungus and its killing millions of bats," explained Wally.

Bradley stopped playing and listened carefully.

"I'm afraid it's affecting every species of bat, Bradley," continued Pete.

"Mother, Father," whispered Bradley.

"It's wiped out entire colonies," commented Wally sadly.

"Grandpa," whispered Bradley, a look of horror growing on his face.

"Bradley," continued Pete, "I'm afraid there's no possible way your family could have survived a plague like this."

"I've gotta go!"

"What? Go where?" Wally asked.

"Home!"

"I say, you can't leave now! There's a blizzard moving in!"

"I've gotta go! Make sure they're all right! Which way is home?"

"Excuse me?" Pete asked in disbelief.

"Which way's home?" Bradley shouted. "Point!"

"It's that way," Wally said nodding to the north.

Bradley took off as fast as he could as Pete and Wally watched with heavy hearts as their friend flew into the darkness.

"Poor little guy," said Wally looking at Pete. "I hope he makes it home okay."

"But what will he find when he gets there?" Pete asked with great concern.

*Bradley flew as fast and as far as he could. He flew from Antarctica, over South America, Mexico, Texas, and New Mexico until finally he reached his cave.*

He cautiously took a look inside and then gasped out loud horrified at what he saw. Thousands of dead bats lay on the floor of the cave. Bradley heard a weak voice from outside of the cave. It was his grandpa Broderick.

"Don't go in there Bradley," Bradley's grandpa warned. "Stay where you are!"

"But Grandpa," Bradley said moving toward his grandpa.

"Don't come any closer Bradley! I've got it too!"

Bradley's heart sank. His eyes started to tear up. He knew this would be the last conversation he'd have with his grandpa.

"Mom and Dad? Are they inside?" Bradley asked, his voice shaking as he pointed to the cave.

"They went to South America to look for you. I'd already caught it so I stayed behind to warn you in case you came back."

"Are Mom and Dad okay?"

"They were when they left. They were just terribly worried about you."

Grandpa Broderick coughed violently and then moaned. Deep down inside Bradley knew that he wouldn't last much longer.

"Sleep, I need to sleep," Grandpa Broderick said full of exhaustion.

Bradley began to cry.

"This is my fault!" Bradley said full of remorse.

"This isn't anybody's fault! You made the choice to go to South America! If you would have stayed here you would have perished with the others!"

"I don't know what to do!"

"Find your parents Bradley, and then fly as far away from here as you can."

"I'm afraid!"

"There's nothing to be afraid of Bradley. Now fly! Always remember the wonderful times we've had together, Bradley. Always remember."

"Don't die Grandpa! I don't want to be alone!"

"You're not alone Bradley. There's someone who will help you."

Grandpa Broderick took one more breath and then life left his body.

Bradley slowly flew from the cave. He was overwhelmed with grief. Not only was he sad about the death of his grandpa, but he was also worried about his parents.

He decided to fly to his favorite thinking tree to rest and think things through.

*As he approached the tree he saw a tiny bat hanging upside down from one of the branches. It was his best friend Brayden.*

"Brayden?" asked Bradley with amazement.

"Bradley? You're alive!" Brayden shouted with joy.

The two best friends were reunited and filled with excitement! They flew and dove in front of the moon just like old times. After catching their breath they hung from a branch of their favorite thinking tree.

"It just set in," Brayden explained. "One day everything was fine and the next everyone started to die. It got my whole family Bradley," Brayden said sadly. "My mom, my dad, my brothers and sisters, they're all gone."

"Why didn't you get it?"

"I flew up into the mountains for a few nights. When I came back, everyone was sick. I stopped by the cave and your grandpa told me what was happening. He told me to leave. I didn't know what to do or where to go so I came here. I'm glad you're alive Bradley."

"I'm glad you're alive too Brayden."

There was a small pause as the two friends went into deep thought.

"What are we going to do now Bradley?"

"I'm going to South America to find my parents!"

Brayden looked sad at the thought of losing his best friend for a second time.

"Come with me!"

"Really?" Brayden asked.

"There's nothing left for you here! Come with me and help me find my parents! You can be a part of our family!"

A huge smile spread across Brayden's face.

"How do we find your parents?" Brayden asked. "South America's a huge place!"

"I have an idea where we can start looking," Bradley said with determination in his voice.

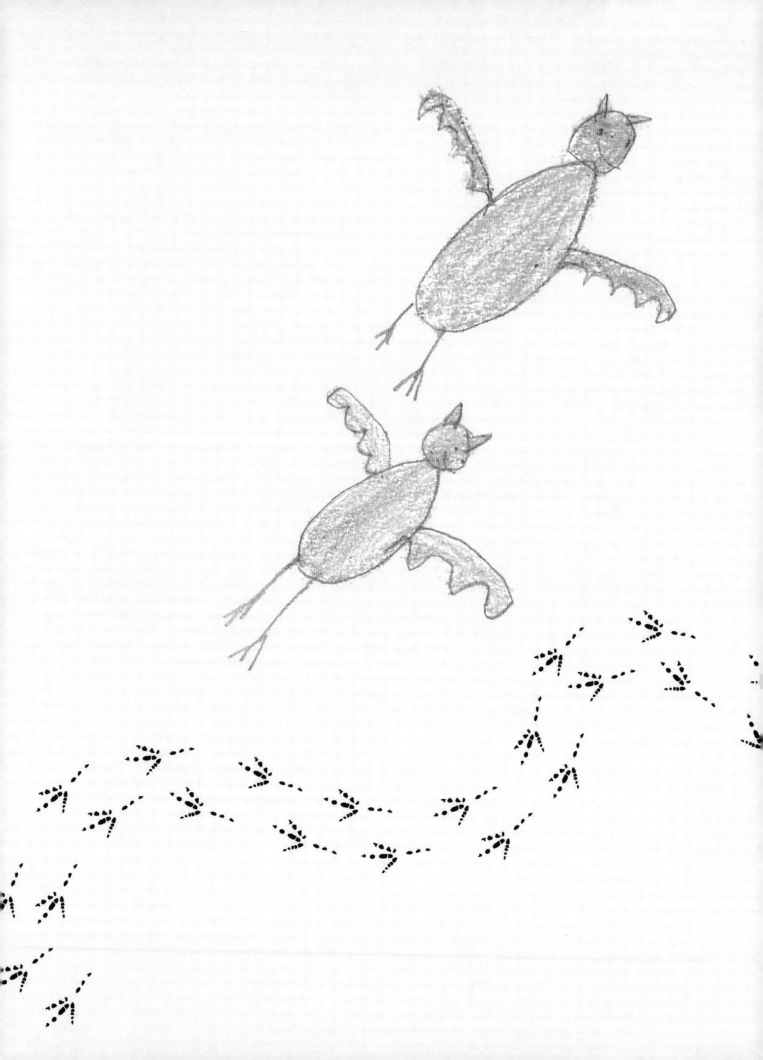

The small fires around the shell of the aeroplane had spread to the surrounding grass and trees. Enormous lightning bolts could be seen in the distance followed by heavy thunder. A gigantic storm was moving across the jungle.

Inside of the plane Victor the Vampire Bat was issuing orders. "Billy! Throw some debris on the fire. It's getting cold in here!"

"B-B-B-But the d-d-d-debris's so heavy," Billy replied.

"Do it now or become my afternoon snack," Victor said grabbing Billy by his wings. "Understood?"

"Y-Y-Y-Yes sir."

Billy groaned as he lifted a small piece of debris and dropped it onto a fire that was burning in one of the corners of the aeroplane.

"I don't like the smell of some of that debris," Fabio said loosening his Kimono.

"Who asked you?" Victor asked rudely. "We've got to keep the fires going!"

A voice is heard from the back of the plane.

"You keep feeding those fires Victor and you're going to set the whole jungle on fire!"

"Then we shall all be consumed in flames! Look who's NOT in a position to talk!"

Victor slowly moved to the back of the plane. Locked inside of a small cage were Bradley's mother and father, Blair and Ben.

"As a matter of fact," Victor continued, "the fires bring in unwitting 'welcome' dinner guests. Like you, if you get what I mean? The light from the fires draw my victims to me."

Suddenly a voice was heard from the front of the plane.

"Let my family go!" shouted Bradley.

"As I was saying," Victor said looking at Bradley's father, "guess who's coming to dinner and guess who's the entree?"

"You heard him," Brayden shouted. "Leave them alone!"

"And looky there," Victor continued, "a side dish!"

"Side dish? Who are you calling a side dish?" shouted Brayden. You're nothing but a rotten old bat!"

Brayden flew to Victor swooping around him kicking him in the head. Billy the Bumblebee Bat flew in front of Bradley trying to block him.

"Y-Y-Y-You can't be here! Victor swore if you ever came back he'd kill you!"

"Out of my way Bee!" Bradley exclaimed.

"I'm s-s-s-serious! He'll k-k-k-kill you!"

"Listen Billy, do you want to get out of here?" whispered Bradley. "And never have to worry about being bullied or being eaten?"

"Well sure, b-b-b-but how?"

"Fly inside the lock hanging on the cage, unlock it, and let my parents out!"

"Victor will s-s-s-see me!"

"We'll take care of old Vic!" exclaimed Bradley. "Just do it!"

Bradley flew toward Brayden and Victor.

An incredible storm began outside of the aeroplane. Sheets of rain fell across the sky as the wind began to howl.

"Leave my friend alone!" shouted Bradley.

"How nice of you to join us for dinner Bradley," observed Victor. "You can watch me dine on the other three before I eat you!"

Both Bradley and Brayden swooped down as fast as they could and continued to kick Victor in the head.

"Ouch! Stop that! Fabio! Get them!" screamed Victor.

"Coming boss!"

"Oh no you don't!" Bradley and Brayden shouted in unison.

Bradley and Brayden flew to Fabio, grabbed the bottom of his Kimono, and wrapped it around his head from behind.

"Hey, what's happening? I can't see! Vic help me!"

The two bats began to kick Fabio in the head. Fabio tripped backward over some debris and fell into the middle of a fire. He began to make sniffing noises through his Kimono.

"Something's burning. Hey that smells pretty good."

Fabio sniffed some more.

"Hey, wait a minute! It's me!"

Fabio let out a huge scream.

"My tush! It's on fire!"

Fabio frantically ran out of the aeroplane and into the jungle, his tush burning brightly.

"I've had quite enough of you two!" Victor said angrily. "Prepare to meet your end!"

Victor slowly approached Bradley and Brayden as Billy flew to the back of the aeroplane and quietly slipped into the key hole.

"I have n-n-n-no idea what I'm d-d-d-doing," said Billy from inside the key hole.

"Billy!"

It was Bradley's father, Ben.

"Put pressure on the pins inside of the lock!" continued Ben.

"D-D-D-Do w-w-w-what?"

"Put pressure on the pins! Push as hard as you can against the pins!"

Billy pushed against the pins with all of his strength. Suddenly he heard a click as the lock fell open.

"I d-d-d-did it! I d-d-d-did it," Billy shouted as he flew out of the lock!

Ben grabbed Billy and put his wing over his mouth.

"Shh," Ben whispered.

Victor, Bradley, and Brayden were in the middle of a terrible fight. Wings, claws, and fangs were flying everywhere. Suddenly the aeroplane shifted, the ground giving way beneath it. Victor hit Brayden and knocked him against the wall of the plane knocking him out cold!

"So much for the mutual admiration society," Victor said grabbing Bradley in his claws.

"Why don't you pick on somebody your own size?" shouted Ben.

"I will as soon as I finish off your son!"

Victor opened his mouth preparing to swallow Bradley whole.

Suddenly the aeroplane shifted again as the ground in front of it gave way. Victor lost his grip on Bradley.

"Blair, get the kids out of the aeroplane while I take care of our host!" shouted Ben.

Blair and Bradley picked up Brayden and flew him outside. Brayden started to regain consciousness as the rain hit his face.

"What happened?" Brayden asked.

"Dad!" Bradley shouted.

Bradley flew to one of the windows and looked inside. Victor was giving Bradley's father a terrible beating. Victor threw Ben from one side of the aeroplane to the other until Ben lay on the floor bloody and exhausted. Billy flew to Ben's side.

"G-G-G-Get out of h-h-h-here or h-h-h-he's going to kill you! Th-Th-Th-There's only one w-w-w-way to take care of him!"

Billy looked up and saw Victor approaching the two of them. Lightning flashed followed by the crashing of thunder.

"Cuchi cuchi coo!" shouted Billy.

Billy flew toward Victor and began to tickle him all over.

"No! No! No! Billy!" Victor screamed with laughter.

Suddenly there was another huge flash of lightning followed by the loudest boom of thunder.

The plane shifted one last time and began to groan loudly as it slid toward the edge of the cliff.

"Dad!" Bradley shouted from outside of the aeroplane. "The cliff''s giving way!"

Ben flew out of a broken window just as the aeroplane fell off the cliff and burst into flames as it hit the ground below.

Bradley and Ben looked over the side of the cliff looking for any sign that Billy had survived the crash. But as time passed they knew they would never see Billy again.

A little while later Bradley and his family were hanging from the branch of a tree. The rain had turned into a slow drizzling mist.

"The rain's put out a lot of the smaller fires," Blair observed.

There was a moment of silence. Everyone was thinking about Billy.

"He was a good bee," Ben commented.

"His name was Billy, Dad," Bradley said, correcting his father.

"He was a good Billy," his father continued.

"He was our hero," continued Brayden. If it wasn't for him we would have all been killed."

"His heart was bigger than he was," commented Blair.

"He was a brave little bat," stated Bradley.

A fifth voice was heard from the edge of the branch.

"H-H-H-Haven't I b-b-b-been through en-n-n-nough without h-h-h-hearing all of t-t-t-this?

"Billy! You're alive," they all shouted!

Bradley's family flew to Billy. Billy's right wing was in a little sling. For over an hour they listened to Billy reenact how he saved every-one. Sometimes the stories were the same, sometimes they weren't. What mattered was that Billy was alive and Victor was gone.

As Bradley's family and Billy flew into the moonlight, a very important conversation was about to take place.

"Mom, Dad, Brayden," Bradley started.

"And B-B-B-Billy," Billy added.

"And Billy," Bradley continued. "I think I know where we should hibernate this year."

"Oh, oh," Brayden warned.

"I think we should go to Africa!"

"Africa?" Ben asked. "How do you know about Africa?"

"A friend told me."

"Where's Africa?" Brayden asked.

"Across the ocean," answered Blair.

"How will we get there?" asked Brayden.

"By ship," answered Bradley.

"Oh n-n-n-no! Billy complained. "I-I-I-I've heard ab-b-b-bout  Africa! It's hot th-th-th-there, and I th-th-th-think th-th-th-there are lions and t-t-t-tigers and b-b-b-bears there!"

"I don't think there are any bears in Africa Billy and listen, your living arrangement in South America wasn't the greatest!" Brayden commented sarcastically.

"Who told you to go by ship?" Bradley's mother asked.

"A friend," Bradley answered with a smile on his face. "A friend."

Bradley the bat will return in *The Wonderful Adventures of Bradley the Bat in Africa.*

# About the Author

**Steve Paulding** was born in Iowa and grew up in Kirksville and Springfield, Missouri. Steve is a graduate of Truman State University. He is the author of the *Life Lessons From Andy Wink* book series. Steve is currently an educator in the Douglas County School District. He lives in Parker, CO where he continues to be inspired by his many students, family, and friends.

# About the Illustrators

**Carter Schmidt** is six years old. He is a first grader at Skyview Academy in Highlands Ranch, Colorado. Carter enjoys chocolate, root beer, art, cooking, camping, learning about rocks, minerals, and tornadoes. Carter is very excited to have illustrated his first book!

**Caleb Schmidt** is nine years old. He is a fourth grader at Skyview Academy in Highlands Ranch, Colorado. Caleb enjoys music, eating, watching football, swimming, reading, and learning about science and math. He hopes everyone enjoys reading about Bradley's adventures!

Made in the USA
Charleston, SC
14 January 2013